D0393714

Nikki & Deja

Substitute Trouble

by Karen English

Illustrated by Laura Freeman

39075043739199

Clarion Books
Houghton Mifflin Harcourt
Boston * New York * 2013

To all the Nikkis and Dejas everywhere
— K.E.
To my Mom, Trudy
— L.F.

Clarion Books
215 Park Avenue South
New York, New York 10003

Clarion Books is an imprint of Houghton Mifflin Harcourt Publishing Company.

www.hmhbooks.com

The text was set in Warnock Pro.
The illustrations were executed digitally.

Library of Congress Cataloging-in-Publication Data
English, Karen.
Nikki and Deja : substitute trouble / by Karen English ; illustrated by Laura Freeman.
p. cm.
Summary: While Ms. Shelby-Ortiz is recovering from an injury, substitute Mr. Willow
takes over Nikki and Deja's third-grade class with disastrous results.
ISBN 978-0-547-61565-3 (hardcover)
[1. Substitute teachers—Fiction. 2. Teachers—Fiction. 3. Behavior—Fiction. 4.
Schools—Fiction. 5. Best friends—Fiction. 6. Friendship—Fiction. 7. African
Americans—Fiction.] I. Freeman-Hines, Laura, ill. II. Title. III. Title: Substitute teacher.
PZ7.E7232Nj 2013
[Fic]—dc23
2012021009

Manufactured in the United States of America
DOC 10 9 8 7 6 5 4 3 2 1
4500415330

– Contents –

1

Where Is Ms. Shelby-Ortiz?

Something not-so-good happens the first Monday after Deja gets her puppy, Ms. Precious Penelope. She wants so much to write about her new pet in her morning journal and then read it to the class when Ms. Shelby-Ortiz asks if there is anyone who would like to share. She pictures herself being one of the only kids to throw a hand up and wave it in the air. Deja imagines reading her entry and Ms. Shelby-Ortiz smiling with approval and surprise that Deja is using so many supporting details and descriptive adjectives. But something not-so-good happens to that picture in her head. Ms. Shelby-Ortiz is not there!

When the whole class is lined up nicely and quietly, waiting to be led into the school, Deja sees an unfamiliar person heading their way across the yard. It's a man! A substitute teacher! Where is Ms. Shelby-Ortiz? Where is their beautiful teacher, who just got married a few months ago and has done that fancy thing with her name (which Deja is going to do with her name too, when she finally grows up and marries)?

The substitute walks right up to the line and stands there in front of the class without saying anything. Nikki, Deja's best friend, looks back at her and frowns. Good. Nikki feels just the same as Deja. That is the good thing about best friends. Most of the time, they feel just like you do.

He holds his hands in front of him and looks up and down the line, as if he's trying to decide who the bad kids are. His eyes stop at Deja for a moment and he seems to look at her more closely, squinting. A few kids behind her begin to whisper to each other. He puts his forefinger over his mouth to quiet them, but real timid-like.

Deja already knows two things. She isn't going to like this sub, and her best friend, Nikki, isn't going to like him either.

As soon as the students enter the classroom and do their morning things — hanging up their coats, putting away their lunches, taking their homework out of their backpacks and putting it in the homework tray on Ms. Shelby-Ortiz's

desk — the new teacher writes his name on the whiteboard in cursive handwriting: *Mr. Willow*.

Too little, Deja thinks. Mr. Willow . . . What kind of name is that, anyway? That's the name of a tree, not a person. He turns around and puts his hands in his pockets.

"My name is Mr. Willow, and I'm going to be your substitute teacher during Ms. Shelby-Ortiz's absence." He says this in a quiet voice without much confidence. Maybe he's new to teaching. He does look pretty young.

Deja doesn't like hearing the word "absence," and she doesn't know why. "Teacher" and "absence" just shouldn't go together. Mr. Willow continues with a little smile on his face like he's secretly happy that Ms. Shelby-Ortiz is *absent*.

"Your teacher had an accident and —"

There's a big, collective gasp. Nikki looks over at Deja. Deja feels her eyes widen. For the past two weeks, Ms. Shelby-Ortiz has been experimenting with letting the kids who usually pay attention sit where they choose. Her only requirement is that they listen when she's talking and that they *stay on task* when they're working. Nikki and Deja have proven that they can do both, so they get to sit at the same table across from each other. Of course.

Mr. Willow holds up his palm. "Hold on, hold on. . . . Your teacher is fine. It's just a broken ankle. She's only going to be out two or three weeks."

Two or three weeks! Deja thinks. *Impossible!*

"A broken ankle!" Carlos calls out, and it sounds like a protest. He often forgets to raise his hand and wait to be recognized before he speaks.

Mr. Willow looks over at him. "It seems she was out walking around her neighborhood— for exercise—and stepped on one of those acorn-type things that fall from trees." Everyone is listening with their full attention. Probably imagining their teacher out walking around for exercise, Deja guesses. And then actually falling and hurting herself.

Nikki raises her hand nicely, and Mr. Willow points at her as if he's a cop directing traffic.

"How did Ms. Shelby-Ortiz get home?" she asks quietly, and Deja wonders if she's going to cry.

"I'm not sure," Mr. Willow says. "But she managed to get to the hospital and have her ankle x-rayed, and it was broken, unfortunately. So she has to spend the next few weeks off her feet. That's why I'm here."

There is a long moment of silence. Deja looks around. It seems as if everyone is busy taking this in. Some are probably imagining Ms. Shelby-Ortiz sitting on her sofa, her foot up on her coffee table with a big cast on it.

"Now, your teacher's husband brought in her lesson-plan book. . . ."

A few kids giggle at the mention of Ms. Shelby-Ortiz's husband. The fact that she now has a husband is still so strange, even for Deja, who was at her wedding.

Mr. Willow goes on. "And a list of the most helpful students."

Deja holds her breath. Has Ms. Shelby-Ortiz noticed how helpful she's been? Especially as lunch monitor and office monitor? Has she noticed how good Deja is at folding her hands and listening *with both ears* when Ms. Shelby-Ortiz is explaining something or giving directions?

Deja glances over at Nikki. She can tell Nikki is waiting too. Mr. Willow is examining a paper in his hand. It must have the names of all the *helpful kids* on it. Deja thinks her name should be at the top of the list.

"Who's Antonia?" Mr. Willow asks, looking around.

Antonia raises her hand straight up. *Like a person reaching for the sky,* Deja thinks.

Antonia smiles to herself and looks over at her best friend, Casey.

This is what Deja can't understand. Why would Antonia be on the list when Deja has had way more jobs? She's sharpened pencils for the teacher, cleaned the whiteboard, and taken the recycling bin out to the big recycle receptacle or whatever it's called. She has, without being asked, arranged the books in the class library. Why, she could go on and on — in her head, of course. And really, what has Antonia done?

"Antonia, it seems you're paper monitor this week."

Antonia frowns at this. She clearly had expected more.

"Carlos? Where's Carlos?"

Carlos shoots his hand up. Deja is surprised. Carlos can't be on the *helpful kids* list!

"You're in charge of keeping the class pencils nice and sharp."

Carlos grins as if he's been given some great job, like office monitor or lunch monitor. Deja shakes her head.

"Who's Deja?" Mr. Willow asks.

Deja shoots her hand up.

"You're book monitor this week." Mr. Willow doesn't even look at her while he says this. He just looks at the paper on the clipboard he has in his hand and calmly checks off something with his pencil. He continues this way until the monitors for the week have been announced. But Deja still can't tell who the *helpful kids* are. Who did Ms. Shelby-Ortiz put on her "helpful" list?

2

Poor Mr. Willow

"I don't like him," Deja tells Nikki at recess. They are sitting on the bench next to the homework table. Since it's Monday, there's no one sitting at the homework table (which is really just a lunch table). The homework table is for the benched kids who didn't do their homework. There's no homework on Fridays, so there are no benched kids on Mondays.

"Why?" Nikki asks.

"Because he doesn't even seem like a real teacher."

"He seems like a real teacher to me."

"Not to me."

"Well," says Nikki, "he just got here. So I don't think you even know what he's like."

"But when we first got into Ms. Shelby's class—"

"Shelby-Ortiz," Nikki corrects.

"Right," Deja says, now a little annoyed about having to say that mouthful every time she wants to talk about Ms. Shelby-Ortiz. "She learned all of our names the first day. But that Mr. *Willow* . . . he hasn't even bothered to learn our names. He says stuff like, 'You in the blue sweater' or 'You with the glasses.' I think that's rude."

Nikki is quiet. Deja wishes she would say something to show that she agrees with her, but she doesn't.

And another thing, Deja concludes after the class has come in from recess and she's able to sit down and really observe Mr. Willow, *Ms. Shelby-Ortiz does not sip coffee from one of those thermal things after recess is over.* Deja bets there's some kind of teacher rule against that. But there he sits on the edge of Ms. Shelby-Ortiz's desk, watching the students take their seats while he sips from his stupid thermos.

"Now," says Mr. Willow, "I'm looking at your teacher's lesson plan and . . ." Then he stops, flustered. "I . . . uh . . ."

Some of the students look at each other and

smile, and Deja picks up an "uh-oh" vibe. She doesn't like the feeling she's getting.

"So, it looks like you're starting a new selection in your reading anthology. 'Three Frogs.'"

Carlos's hand goes up. "We read that last week," he says.

Deja's mouth drops open. Nikki's does as well. Deja looks behind her. Some of the kids have secretive smirks on their faces. Some look concerned.

"Oh," Mr. Willow says. "I thought . . ." His voice drifts off.

"We're on 'Smoke Signals,'" Richard calls out without raising his hand. Deja doesn't like what's going on. It's the way some kids act when there's a substitute. They do things they would *never* do with their regular teacher.

Mr. Willow looks through his big teacher's edition. "Okay, everyone . . . Turn to page fifty-seven. We'll be reading 'Smoke Signals' instead." He looks up from the book and squints. He glances around. Then something dawns on Deja. Mr. Willow wears glasses. It's probably time for a new pair. "You, in the green sweater. You can go first."

Luckily, it's Beverly. She's never a problem. She always does exactly as she's told. Even though she knows the class is on "Three Frogs," Mr. Willow said to read "Smoke Signals," so "Smoke Signals" it will be.

She begins in a halting voice because she's not a very good reader. Mr. Willow has to tell her some of the easiest words, like *Native* and *American*. For Deja, this is the hardest part about reading round-robin style. When someone isn't a very good reader, he or she takes forever to get through just one paragraph, and Deja almost feels as if she's going to fall asleep. But Beverly does reach the end, and Deja shoots her hand up so that she can be the next reader. She's dying to show Mr. Willow what a good reader sounds like. But he's got some notion in his head that the next reader should be a boy.

Too bad he calls on Carlos. Carlos is ready. Deja doesn't know what he's going to pull, but she knows it's going to be something. He begins to read in a nice, clear voice, not having any problems with the so-called big words. But when she looks down in her book to follow along, she finds he's skipped two paragraphs and is reading the paragraph near the bottom of the page.

Mr. Willow realizes this at the same time and attempts to stop Carlos. "Wait, wait. . . . I think you're on the wrong paragraph."

Mistake Number One. Actually, it's Mistake

Number Ten, Deja thinks. Mr. Willow should have said very clearly, "You're on the wrong paragraph. Go up to paragraph two." And then he should have looked at Carlos very sternly. But instead he starts off with, "I think . . ." Deja shakes her head slowly.

Carlos looks up innocently. He even raises both eyebrows and widens his eyes. And some of the boys in the class clearly think the fact that he's gotten away with this so easily is the greatest fun in the world.

Luckily, Mr. Willow calls on the new boy, Gavin, next. He's one of the good kids and he's really smart, too. He begins to read the paragraph that follows the one Mr. Willow had directed Carlos to read. He reads smoothly and calmly. Some from the Knucklehead Club—as Nikki and Deja call the kids who can never stay on task and do what they're supposed to do— look at him with scowls on their faces, annoyed that the new boy isn't going along with the fun.

Ayanna makes up for it. When Mr. Willow calls on her, she reads in a voice so soft, she can hardly be heard.

"Can you speak up a little bit?" Mr. Willow asks.

Mistake Number Zillion, Deja thinks. He should have said, "Speak up, or I'll have to call on someone else." Then if she continues in that baby voice, he should look around and ask, "Who in this class has a nice loud voice?" Even the boys' hands would have shot up. They would have wanted to outdo everyone else. They would have forgotten all about their silly game.

For a sentence or so, Ayanna does read in a regular voice, but then little by little her voice returns to a near whisper until Carlos raises his hand while calling out at the same time, "I can't hear her! I don't know where we are!"

Mr. Willow is noticeably flustered. "Why don't we just do silent reading and then answer the questions at the end of the selection?"

Mistake Number Zillion and Three, according to Deja: Don't ask. *Tell.*

Students begin to take out their workbooks. A couple of kids get out of their seats — without permission — to sharpen their pencils. They would *never* do that if Ms. Shelby-Ortiz was there. That makes Deja angry the most. Some kids hold their pencils in the sharpener too long, and they know good and well Ms. Shelby-Ortiz has cautioned them against doing that. "You can burn out the motor like that," she has told them. Some sharpen, look at their point, sharpen, look at their point again . . . just wasting time. Mr. Willow looks over at the line at the pencil sharpener, and Deja can tell it makes him feel uneasy. She can also tell he doesn't know what to do about it.

She just has to come to his rescue. She raises her hand and waves it around a bit to get his attention. He looks over at her. "Yes, uh . . ."

"I'm Deja," she says. "Mr. Willow, Ms. Shelby-Ortiz doesn't let a whole bunch of kids get up at the same time to sharpen their pencils."

"She doesn't?"

"No, what she does is ask people to raise their hands if they need to sharpen their pencils. Then she gives the kids who have raised their hands a number like one, two, three . . . like that. And then they have to go in that order, but they can't go until it's their number."

Mr. Willow looks as if he's really trying hard to follow what Deja's saying. She goes on.

"And when there's a kid who keeps breaking their pencil lead because they just want to get up and not do their work, then she gives them one of those big fat kindergarten pencils. Because nobody can break that lead. They're in her top drawer," Deja says finally. She notes Carlos has turned around to give her a dirty look, but she doesn't care.

Mr. Willow opens Ms. Shelby-Ortiz's desk drawer. He takes out three kindergarten pencils. Deja just knows that there were some kids who'd planned to pull that broken-pencil routine. She smiles to herself. But then she notices that Carlos is sitting next to his good friend Ralph in Ayanna's seat. She's tempted to tell that, too, but she doesn't want to seem like a real tattletale, so she says nothing.

She says nothing even when Keisha *and* Ayanna ask to go to the restroom. They know Ms. Shelby-Ortiz never lets friends go to the restroom together. They just want to get out to play. And if it's close to the time to line up for lunch, Ms. Shelby-Ortiz makes a person wait. Unless it's an emergency. Last month Beverly didn't tell Ms. Shelby-Ortiz that it was an emergency. She just raised her hand calmly and then, upon getting permission, left the classroom for the restroom. When she didn't come back, Ms. Shelby-Ortiz sent Deja to go and find out what happened.

Deja found her in a stall with wet clothes. Poor Beverly had to be escorted (with Deja's jacket tied around her waist) to the nurse's office, where her mother had to be called to bring dry clothes. It was a secret between Deja and Ms. Shelby-Ortiz and Beverly. Deja felt special having that secret. Of course, she eventually broke down and told Nikki, but only after swearing her to secrecy.

"I don't like the way the class is acting," Deja says to Nikki as they leave the lunch table to walk toward the tetherball courts — Room Ten's area for the week.

"Me, neither," Nikki agrees. "They would never do that kind of stuff if Ms. Shelby-Ortiz was here."

"I'm going to tell her," Deja says. "I'm going to tell her about all the kids who were acting bad and all the things they did while she was gone." She looks over at Nikki. "Let's keep a record. We can use our morning journals, since we have to write in them every morning."

Suddenly, Nikki gasps and puts her hand over her mouth. "We didn't do our morning journals!"

"We'll have to remind Mr. Willow about our morning journals tomorrow," Deja says.

The afternoon is worse than the morning. During silent reading, Carlos throws a spitball at the back of Beverly's head. It lands on her desk.

"Yuck!" Beverly screams, and jumps up out of her chair.

Mr. Willow, who's writing something on the board, turns quickly. His eyes dart around, but Carlos is back to looking innocent, staring down at his open book.

"Someone threw a spitball at me!" Beverly cries. She glares down at it as if it's the grossest thing she's ever seen.

"Who did that?" Mr. Willow asks. Deja hears a bit of a shaky tone in his voice.

No one speaks. Mr. Willow looks around the room. Finally, he goes back to putting sentences on the board.

Then, as Deja knew he would, Richard works on his own spitball and shoots it at Beverly. It lands in her hair.

She grabs the back of her head, pulls out the spitball, then screams as she throws it down.

"Ewww," she yells. "Eww, eww, eww!" She looks as if she's going to cry.

The whole class begins to laugh loudly.

Deja suppresses her own laughter. It *is* funny watching Beverly jump around.

"Class!" Mr. Willow says, his face growing red and his voice only slightly raised. "If this doesn't stop, we . . . I . . . I . . . we might not be able to have Physical Education, P.E., today!"

Only a few kids calm down. The Knucklehead Club ignores him. They keep up the loud laughter.

"Whoever threw that . . . that spitball . . ."

More laughter starts up.

"I want them to stop and — and put that thing in the trash!"

"I have to wash my hands!" Beverly cries. "I have to wash my hands!"

"Yes, go," Mr. Willow says. "You have my permission." He looks around the class. "I want no more of that spitball throwing."

The laughter gets louder and Mr. Willow gets redder. "Or there'll be no — no P.E."

Again the laughter dies down a little bit, but some kids keep it going.

If only Ms. Shelby-Ortiz could see them now, Deja thinks.

The horsing around never completely stops. A coughing chorus starts up after P.E., led by Richard. He coughs, and when he stops, another kid takes it up, and then another kid and another, until finally Mr. Willow looks up suspiciously from correcting papers. The kickball game during P.E. is a fiasco too. There is lots of arguing over who's going to roll the ball for the kicker and over whether someone is out or not. It is a mess.

Dismissal is horrible. The bell rings and there's a rush to the door. Mr. Willow looks at the crush helplessly and seems to throw up his hands. He walks over, opens the door, and lets everyone out.

"Ms. Shelby-Ortiz would never have let the class out," Deja complains to Nikki as they walk home from school. "She would have made everyone go back to their seats and then she'd have someone recite the rules about dismissal and then let us go one at a time."

"Yeah," Nikki says sadly.

"We should write Mr. Willow a note about how things are supposed to be."

Nikki seems to be thinking about this for a moment. "Kids are going to get mad at us for being goody-goods."

Deja rolls her eyes. "So?" Then she says, "We can do it anon . . . anon . . ." Deja can't remember the word exactly.

"Anonymously," Nikki says easily.

Deja's not surprised. Nikki plans to be a journalist when she grows up. She knows a lot of words that Deja doesn't. Words are very important to Nikki.

Deja has three things to do when she gets home: Feed Ms. Precious Penelope (or, as Deja's Auntie has begun to call the dog, Ms. P.), walk Ms. Precious Penelope, and do her homework. It was Auntie Dee who saved Ms. P. from getting run over by a car. She'd seen the small brown dog with the long thin legs and pointy little face trapped on the median on Crocker Boulevard, a super-busy street. She'd parked her car, and when it was safe, she had run across the street to where Ms. P. was stuck, grabbed her, and carried her back to the car. She went straight to the pound, where the pound lady said if no one claimed the dog in seven days, Auntie Dee could keep her.

"I didn't even know I wanted a dog," Auntie Dee told her best friend, Phoebe, on the phone, "until I saw this poor little helpless thing—all scared and shivering and not able to go forward or backward." Auntie told Phoebe that she suddenly wanted to take the dog home. She just didn't know what had come over her.

They waited the seven days and no one claimed Ms. Penelope. Auntie Dee thought someone had abandoned her. Anyway, Ms. P. is a nice addition to their home, and so easy. If you don't count the occasional *accidents* in the house, that is. Deja loves Ms. Penelope as much as she once loved Bear, her favorite stuffed animal that she's recently outgrown. *Where is Bear, anyway?* she thinks.

"When do you want to work on the anonymous letter to poor Mr. Willow?" Nikki asks.

"I have to walk Ms. Precious Penelope first and feed her and do my homework. I'll come over after that."

Auntie Dee is doing freelance work at home until she can go back to her very fun job at the theater company. The company ran out of money—for now—so they had to "let Auntie Dee go." Deja's happy that Auntie Dee has enough work that things haven't changed too much. There's no money for "extras," but Deja hasn't had much need for extras. Maybe extras will be more important later. And when they become important, the theater company will call Auntie Dee back to work.

Auntie Dee is in front of her computer when Deja comes through the front door.

"Hi, honey," she calls out. "I already walked Ms. P. for you, and she's been fed."

"Can I take her over to Nikki's for a little bit and do my homework over there?"

"I guess so," Auntie Dee says, and then squints at the computer screen.

3

Dear Mr. Willow

Nikki loves Ms. P. almost as much as Deja does. And Ms. P. loves anyone who will stroke her under the chin. So while they sit on Nikki's porch thinking of the perfect anonymous letter, they take turns petting Ms. P., who seems to be drifting off to sleep.

"How should we start?" Deja asks Nikki, who has her special pad on her lap and her pencil poised over it.

"Hmm," Nikki says, thinking. "I know. When my mother has me write letters to my great-aunt Nora, she tells me to start with, 'I hope this letter finds you well. . . .'"

Deja thinks about this. "But would we be wanting to find him . . . *well?* That sounds funny. He might wonder what we mean by that."

"No," says Nikki. "He'll probably be grateful that someone hopes he's well."

Deja shakes her head impatiently. "What next?"

"We just tell him why we are writing to him."

"Like . . . ?" Deja needs specifics.

"Hold on," Nikki says. She's busy writing something. Deja waits. Tiny little Ms. P. yawns wide in her sleep.

"Okay, how does this sound?" Nikki begins to read:

"Dear Mr. Willow,
We hope this letter finds you well. There is some stuff that went on today in our class that you probably don't know about. There's some bad kids in our class who haven't been doing what they're supposed to do. And they've been telling you the wrong stuff a lot. Like Richard and Carlos was reading the wrong paragraphs on purpose and we really did have to read Three Frogs and Carlos wasn't in the right seat and kids know they weren't supposed to be sharpening their pencils like they were. We think you should tell Ms. Shelby-Ortiz all this stuff when she gets back. And you should probably bench the bad kids or tell them you're going to bench

them to make them act good. Because we know they can act good because they act good when Ms. Shelby-Ortiz is here. And Carlos and Richard were the ones who threw those spitballs.

Signed,
Anonymous

"So, what do you think?" Nikki asks, looking at her letter as if she's really proud of it.

"It's good," Deja says. "Do you want to do our homework out here with Ms. P.?"

"Sure," Nikki says. She goes into the house to get her books and a notebook.

Deja looks over at Ms. P., who seems to be twitching through a dream.

On the way to school the next morning, Deja thinks of something. "Nikki, if this is supposed to be anon . . . anon . . ."

"Anonymous," Nikki says.

"Yes, anonymous . . . Then how do we get it to Mr. Willow?"

"Hmm," Nikki says. "We can put it on his desk—"

"Ms. Shelby-Ortiz's desk."

"Right. Ms. Shelby-Ortiz's desk. When he's not looking."

"You think we can get away with that?"

Nikki shrugs.

Deja sighs. Since Nikki wrote the letter, it's Deja's job to deliver it. It's going to be tricky.

Mr. Willow is standing at the head of the line when Deja and Nikki walk onto the school-yard. He has a clipboard in his hand. He uses it to see if everyone is where he or she should be. But already Carlos and Ralph and Richard and Keisha are in the wrong places and laughing to themselves. The sight of them makes Deja angry. She and Nikki quietly get in their places and wait for the bell to ring, the one that tells everyone it's time to go to class. Mr. Willow walks behind the students as they file into the building. Ms. Shelby-Ortiz always leads them. At certain spots, she stops to see if everyone is lined up correctly and walking in an orderly fashion.

As soon as the class enters Room Ten, they scatter. Everyone knows the morning routine, but some hang out at the cubbies, taking their time and socializing. Some gather around each other's desks. Mr. Willow gave a little bit of homework the day before, but the homework basket is only half full. Deja looks around and her anger grows. Nikki looks like she's not liking what she's seeing, either.

Mr. Willow goes to the light switch and turns it on and off and on and off. Most of the students stop then and look at him to see what that's about.

"Uh, class, can we put our homework in the basket and get in our seats?"

Deja wonders why he is talking like that. He shouldn't ask and he shouldn't include himself. He should just tell the class what to do and follow that up with threats. She's tempted to yell out, "Everybody, get in your SEATS!" But she doesn't.

Eventually the people who are fooling around drift toward their desks and sit down. Ms. Shelby-Ortiz had gotten rid of their rows and now has them sitting in cooperative groups of four desks facing each other. Mr. Willow stands at the front of the room and asks the students to state their names. Carlos says his name is Ralph and Ralph says his name is Carlos, then everyone bursts into laughter and Mr. Willow looks flustered.

Richard gets up to sharpen his pencil, and when Mr. Willow says, "You in the blue shirt, please get back in your—" Richard interrupts him.

"My name is not 'You in the blue shirt.' It's Richard."

Everyone freezes in place. The room falls silent. This is one of those moments Auntie Dee talks about — when you can hear a pin drop. Richard has just talked back to a grownup, a teacher. Never in a thousand years would he have said that to Ms. Shelby-Ortiz. Never.

"Richard, please return to your seat."

Deja thinks Ms. Shelby-Ortiz would have said, "Richard, either get back in your seat or stay in for recess. The choice is yours." Then she would have stared him down until he obeyed.

But Mr. Willow doesn't even look like he means what he says.

The morning doesn't go well. Mr. Willow has them take out their morning journals and write about a favorite item they have in their bedroom. Half of the class is talking and breaking their pencil leads on purpose and generally wasting time.

Next, Mr. Willow puts sentences on the board with mistakes for them to correct. When he turns around to look at the class, Deja raises her hand.

"Yes?" he says.

"May I sharpen my pencil, Mr. Willow?" She said *may* instead of *can,* and she hopes he notices.

"Certainly," he says. He turns back to the board.

Deja gets up to go to the pencil sharpener. On her way there, she glances around to make sure no one is watching, then puts the folded letter on Ms. Shelby-Ortiz's desk. Right in the center. Right where Mr. Willow will be sure to see it.

Dismissal for morning recess is extra disorderly. When the bell rings, Keisha and Rosario jump up out of their seats and run to the door that lets out onto the yard. Of course, all the copycats jump up out of their seats to do the same, until there's a big rush at the door. Only the good kids stay in their seats: Gavin and Erik and Nikki and Deja and Beverly and a few others. Mr. Willow is so caught off-guard and flustered, he can barely get his words out.

"Uh ... Hey, wait a minute. I haven't dismissed anyone. Everyone has to line up first. I need this class lined up. . . ." The kids at the door push it open and run out as if they haven't even heard him. Deja and Nikki, at Table Three, get out of their seats and line up at the door along with all those who've chosen to follow Mr. Willow's instructions. Instead of calling the errant kids back, which is what Ms. Shelby-Ortiz would do (boy, would those kids get it!), he just follows them outside and stands there a moment watching after them and looking helpless.

Deja is totally disgusted. She wishes she

could just call up Ms. Shelby-Ortiz and tell her all about what's happening in her class during her absence, but she doesn't have her telephone number.

"Maybe he'll do something when he reads our anonymous note," Nikki says. They're headed for the jump-rope area. Keisha and Ayanna are already there in line, waiting their turns.

"Why are you guys being bad with Mr. Willow?" Deja asks as soon as she takes her place behind them.

"What?" Ayanna asks in an innocent voice.

"You know what," Nikki says, joining in. "You'd never do all that bad stuff if Ms. Shelby-Ortiz was here."

Ayanna rolls her eyes and turns back around.

"I think Mr. Willow should write Ms. Shelby-Ortiz a report and tell her everything you guys have been doing," Deja says.

Ayanna just shrugs, then jumps into the turning ropes and begins chanting, *All last night and the night before, twenty-four robbers came knocking at the door. . . .*

4

Kick Me!

Later, before the class drifts into Room Ten— the line has completely fallen apart — Deja over- hears something horrid. She hears Carlos tell Richard he's going to sneak a Post-it onto Mr. Willow's jacket. And it's going to say "Kick Me."

As soon as Deja enters the classroom, she looks at the teacher closely. She wishes she knew what to do. Then she remembers their anony- mous letter. She looks over at Mr. Willow to see if he seems to have read it. She can't tell. He's standing by the whiteboard with Ms. Shelby- Ortiz's teacher's edition, looking like he's wait- ing for everyone to settle down so that he can explain their workbook assignment.

The class makes him wait a long time. Not

Deja and Nikki and Gavin and Erik and Beverly and Antonia, though. They all sit with their hands folded on their desks. Deja looks over at Richard. He has sneaked a Post-it off the pad on Ms. Shelby-Ortiz's desk and has written "Kick Me!" on it in red marker. He's holding it up so Carlos can see.

Quickly, Deja scribbles a note to Nikki, then coughs to get her attention. It's the signal they sometimes use when passing notes to each other. Nikki looks over at Deja and sees her putting the folded paper in the box of markers and colored pencils and crayons that sits in the middle of Table Three. Each group of four desks has a box of shared art supplies in the center. Nikki takes the note out and opens it on her lap. It reads:

Carlos and Richard are going to put a sticky note on the back of Mr. Willow's jacket and it's going to say Kick Me.

Nikki's mouth drops open. She refolds the paper and puts it in her desk.

"All right, class," Mr. Willow begins. "Let's take our Language Arts workbooks out, and can we turn to page forty-two?" He goes on to explain the assignment and then makes the mistake of

asking if there are any questions. Ralph's hand shoots up.

"Yes, uh . . . Ralph." He's been making an effort to learn everyone's name, at least.

"I don't get it."

"What is it you don't understand?"

"What are we supposed to do?"

"You're going to underline the subject of each sentence once and the predicate twice."

"What's a predicate?"

Deja's hand flies up.

"Yes, uh . . ."

"It's Deja, Mr. Willow."

"Oh, yes. Deja?"

"Ms. Shelby-Ortiz taught us all about predicates last week. And we had lots of practice. Ralph wasn't paying attention. He never pays attention and he's always asking for help 'cause he wants the teacher to do the work for him."

It's a mouthful, and she nearly runs out of breath. The whole class has turned to stare at her, even Antonia, who has put herself squarely in the good-kid group by being super obedient.

"Thank you, Deja," Mr. Willow says. "So, anyone who needs extra help, you can join me at the kidney-shaped table."

At least ten of Nikki and Deja's classmates stand up and carry their chairs to the kidney-shaped teacher table. They have to bunch up, and this causes a logjam around the table. Mr. Willow squeezes through a small opening between chairs and settles himself in the part of the table that curves inward.

Deja shakes her head and gets to work.

Then the most awful thing happens. Right before lunch, Deja sees the "Kick Me!" Post-it stuck to the back of Mr. Willow's jacket as he's writing the week's spelling words on the board. Someone must have put it there when everyone was crowded around the teacher table.

Kids are snickering, and not even under their breath. Mr. Willow turns around with a puzzled look on his face. He scans the room, but suddenly all the kids have returned to their workbooks to give the impression that nothing's going on. When he turns back to the board, the laughter begins again. Deja looks over at Nikki, whose eyes have grown big and who has her hand over her mouth. Deja wants to scream, "Stop it!" What they are doing is mean, and Auntie Dee has always told her how most people get up in the morning hopeful and wanting to do their best. When a person is mean, it's because they've forgotten that or they don't know it in the first place. Thinking about Mr. Willow putting on his jacket that morning, not knowing that some bad kid was going to put a mean Post-it on it, makes Deja want to cry.

Mr. Willow continues writing on the board. Then, miracle of miracles, he takes off his jacket, without looking away from what he's writing. He places it on Ms. Shelby-Ortiz's desk. If only she could get to that jacket, Deja thinks. She is pondering the ways she might do this when Richard begins his stupid cough thing. At first, no one pays attention. Mr. Willow does not even look up. But then Carlos coughs too. Still, that seems okay. No one pays attention. All the students just continue writing in their workbooks. Then Richard coughs again.

Deja looks up with suspicion. She looks around the classroom. Nikki is frowning and looking around also. Antonia and Casey glance over at Carlos and then Richard. Antonia rolls her eyes and gets back to her workbook.

Richard coughs a third time, and then Ralph coughs twice.

Now Carlos, Richard, and Ralph start up a coughing chorus. Ayanna joins them, and Keisha gets in on it as well.

Mr. Willow looks around. "I want everyone who's doing that coughing to stop. Right now."

The coughing stops. But in four or five minutes, another version of it starts up. Ralph tests a little cough, more like a loud clearing of the throat. Richard clears his throat next, and then Ayanna.

Mr. Willow just shakes his head and continues writing on the board, apparently deciding to ignore it, but more and more kids join in and it gets harder and harder to ignore all that clearing of throats.

"I'd like to see some order," Mr. Willow says feebly.

Some of the kids do show him some order. That's when Deja gets her idea.

She looks at the jacket in a little pile on the desk. She notices her letter sticking out of the pocket. He *has* read it! She glances over at Nikki. Nikki has returned to her workbook, but she must feel Deja's stare because she looks up and meets Deja's eyes. Deja points to Mr. Willow's jacket with the letter sticking out of the pocket. Nikki mouths, "Wow."

Deja knows just how she's going to get that Post-it note off Mr. Willow's jacket before he can see it. She raises her hand, and when Mr. Willow notices, he looks relieved that someone is actually following the rules.

"May I sharpen my pencil again? The lead broke."

"Why, certainly," he tells Deja, and then goes

back to writing more spelling words on the board.

Deja starts across the room with her pencil. It doesn't really need sharpening, but it's a good excuse. Just as she's lifting Mr. Willow's jacket to get the Post-it note off, Carlos says, very rudely and very loudly, "Hey, Mr. Willow, can I go to the bathroom?" The teacher turns around, and his eyes zoom in on Deja with the Post-it in one hand and her other hand on his jacket.

"What are you doing?" he asks. Suddenly he looks very tired.

"I — I," she stammers, not knowing what to say.

Mr. Willow steps toward her quickly. He takes the note out of her hand, reads it, and then looks at Deja with an expression that's full of sadness. His shoulders slump. "This is serious, I'm afraid. Who's office monitor?" He looks around. Everyone is stunned into silence. Rosario raises her hand with a scared look on her face. Mr. Willow writes a long note on a piece of paper. It seems to take forever for him to finish. "Please take Deja and this note to the office. Ask Mrs. Marker in the office to give the note to the principal."

"Mr. Willow —" Nikki starts. But Mr. Willow holds up his hand and looks so serious, she stops midsentence.

"Please take Deja to the office."

Deja doesn't know what to say, so she decides to say nothing. Actually, it's going to be better to explain everything to Mr. Brown, the principal. So she follows Rosario out of the room. She's sure she'll be able to explain the true situation to Mr. Brown, *easily.*

Mrs. Marker is busy with a parent when they get to the office, so they have to stand in front of the counter in silence for a long time. Then after the parent leaves, the phone rings and they get to listen to Mrs. Marker's conversation, which is pretty interesting. Someone's home on suspension and Mrs. Marker is trying to explain to the parent that the only way the student can come back is when the parent has a meeting with the teacher. She has to explain this over and over in different ways. Deja finds it really interesting, and by the way Rosario is standing there with just her eyes moving, she knows Rosario finds it interesting as well.

Finally Mrs. Marker gets off the phone and looks down at them. Rosario hands her the Post-it and the note from Mr. Willow, and she reads them. "Okay, Miss Rosario, you can go back to class, and Deja, you can have a seat and wait for Mr. Brown to speak with you."

Before Rosario goes, she hands Mrs. Marker something else. It's the letter Nikki and Deja had written. Deja is surprised. She hadn't noticed Mr. Willow giving it to Rosario. She's puzzled, too. Why did he think the letter had anything to do with her? They had given it to Mr. Willow *anonymously.* Deja sits down to wait.

Soon, she's ushered into Mr. Brown's office. There are pictures of Mr. Brown at different school events. In one he's holding a huge pumpkin; in another he's handing a kid the spelling-bee champion trophy. She takes the seat in front of his desk and looks around. Mr. Brown is busy reading the note from Mr. Willow that Mrs. Marker has given him. He picks up the Post-it and turns it over in his hand. There's a picture of a woman and two kids on Mr. Brown's desk, angled toward Deja just enough that she can kind of see them. She guesses that they are his wife and children. Deja thinks about that for a moment.

"Well," he finally says. "My, my, my, and I thought I'd seen everything."

Deja frowns.

"In all my years, I've never seen such an example of disrespect."

Deja's not sure what he means, but she's sure it's not good.

"I can't imagine what you must be thinking to try and pull something like this." He holds up the Post-it with a really disgusted look on his face. "Putting this on the back of your teacher's jacket. This is very, very serious."

Deja starts to protest, but Mr. Brown holds up his hand.

"And it seems," he continues, "you and the rest of the class have been doing everything you can to show your teacher disrespect and to give this school a bad name."

"But Mr. Brown, I didn't do anything. I was just trying to help." Deja finally found her voice.

"Are you saying you didn't have this Post-it in your hand?"

"Yes, I mean, no, I mean . . ." Deja is so flustered she doesn't know what she's trying to say. "I was taking it *off* his jacket," she finally blurts out. "And it was Nikki and me who wrote that letter to Mr. Willow and put it on his desk. That other note Mrs. Marker gave you."

"Really?" Mr. Brown says. He looks at her closely as if he doesn't believe her, but then he says, "You know, I've never had any problems with you, Deja. I know your aunt is hard working, while at the same time trying to raise you with good values. But I'm finding it hard to believe that this letter is from you, and that you had nothing to do with the Post-it with such strong evidence against you."

"Mr. Brown, Nikki and me . . . we wrote that letter yesterday and put it on Ms. Shelby-Ortiz's desk this morning for Mr. Willow to find."

"How can I know that's what happened?"

"Mr. Brown, you can ask Rosario. Mr. Willow gave the letter to her to give to Mrs. Marker. I never opened it, but I know what's in it."

Mr. Brown opens the letter. "Okay. Tell me what it says."

Deja remembers it word for word. She begins: *"Dear Mr. Willow, We hope this letter finds you well. There's some stuff that went on today in our class that you probably don't know about. . . ."*

Deja recites the entire letter, ending with: *"Signed, Anonymous."*

Mr. Brown is smiling when she finishes. He stares out the window for a moment. Then he says, "I have a solution to this problem, but I need to speak to your substitute first. I think we can get this all straightened out." He finds a blank paper, takes a while to write something on it, folds it in half, and then staples it. "You may go back to your class. Please give this to your teacher."

Deja takes the note, wondering what's in it. But the staple keeps her prying eyes from finding out.

As she walks down the hall, it feels as if every person who looks up to see her go by knows that she's just come from the principal's office. She feels guilty, though she's done nothing wrong. And when she enters her classroom, all activity stops and everyone looks her way. Deja sees that Mr. Willow had been letting the class make get-well cards for Ms. Shelby-Ortiz. The room was noisy as she approached the door. Now, once again, you could hear a pin drop.

She walks straight over to where Mr. Willow sits at the desk correcting work and hands him the note from Mr. Brown. Everyone watches her with interest. Then they watch him.

He reads the note and nods at Deja. "You may go back to your seat, Deja."

"Can I get some paper to make Ms. Shelby-Ortiz a get-well card?"

Mr. Willow nods again and goes back to correcting papers.

At the art table, Deja gets a tube of glitter that already has the glue in it, along with markers and construction paper — purple, since that's the closest color to lavender, and lavender is Deja's favorite color. The class seems to have lost a bit of its bluster. Carlos looks over at her nervously, perhaps wondering what she told Mr. Brown. Deja thinks the Knucklehead Club probably realizes it went too far. Because now Mr. Brown knows there's a problem in Room Ten.

It's a relief when the dismissal bell rings. Half the class jumps up and starts going to the cubbies without permission, grabbing their backpacks, and running to the door. Some even push and shove.

"I'd like to see some order," Mr. Willow says feebly.

Deja and Nikki gather their backpacks and wait for Mr. Willow to say, "Okay, you may go."

"I'd like to see some order," Mr. Willow says again.

A few of the kids do show him some order.

"Okay, you may go," he says.

5

A Change Is Coming

"What happened in the principal's office?" Nikki asks the second they leave the schoolyard, as if the question is about to make her burst.

"I didn't get into trouble," Deja says. "'Cause I proved that we were the ones who had tried to help Mr. Willow. That we were the ones who wrote that letter."

"How did you do that?" Nikki asks.

"I knew what was in it. Even the part that said, *I hope this letter finds you well.*"

Nikki is quiet, thinking about this.

As they near their houses, Deja gets a little bubble of excitement in her stomach. She gets to walk Ms. Penelope today. Auntie Dee promised she would save Ms. P.'s walk for Deja.

"You want to do homework at my house?" Nikki asks as she heads up the walkway toward her porch.

"I'm going to walk Ms. Penelope first."

"Can I come?" Nikki asks.

"Sure. We just have to be back in thirty minutes."

They decide to walk up to Marin, then over to Ashby, then down to Maynard, and then back to Fulton, their own street. "That way, we can go by Mr. Delvecchio's and get some hot pops," Deja says. Her mouth waters at the thought of the cinnamon and ginger suckers that are round like Ping-Pong balls, only a little bit smaller.

Ms. Precious Penelope trots along ahead of them, occasionally pulling at her leash, sometimes stopping to sniff the grass. Deja feels happy walking her dog.

"Let me have the leash," Nikki says.

Deja passes it to her reluctantly. "You can walk her for a little bit."

Ms. Precious Penelope seems to sense the change and looks back and then stops.

"I think she likes just me to walk her."

"Dogs don't care who walks them. They just like to be walked."

"How do you know? You've never had a dog."

Nikki doesn't answer. She holds the leash tightly when Ms. P. starts up again, as if she's worried Deja might take it back.

"Let's go through the park," Deja says.

"But we have to be back in thirty minutes," Nikki reminds her.

"Going through the park is a shortcut."

Nikki and Deja turn in the direction of the park.

"I was thinking about something, Deja."

Deja notices Nikki is keeping her face straight ahead, so it's probably some kind of criticism. "What is it now?"

"I think you should call Ms. Penelope *Miss* Penelope."

"Why?"

"Because how can a dog be a Ms.? That's what women call themselves so nobody'll know if they're married or not."

Deja frowns. "I like *Ms.* better than *Miss.* Just like Ms. Shelby-Ortiz. She's married now and she's still a Ms. *Ms.* is better. A dog can be a Ms."

They come to the corner, stop, and look both ways up and down the empty street before crossing.

The park is full of joggers and skateboarders and bikers, and little kids who don't have to worry about homework. They're playing on the monkey bars and in the sandbox with their mothers nearby on benches. Ms. Penelope gets so excited to be in the midst of so much activity, she starts yapping loudly and trying to run off. Nikki holds on to the leash.

"Let me have the leash now," Deja says.

Ms. Penelope seems to know when the leash is back in Deja's hand. She settles down and prances along calmly, looking this way and that.

Suddenly Nikki stops. She shields her eyes. "Is that Mr. Willow?"

Deja follows her gaze and sees Mr. Willow ahead of them on the path, walking a big, bull-headed, ferocious-looking dog. It's one of those dogs that are built low to the ground. Mr. Willow is out of his usual school clothes — slacks and a crisply ironed shirt — and has on some kind of athletic wear. Not only is he walking a dog that looks like it would love to bite someone, right beside him is a young woman with a ponytail and one of those terry-cloth headbands.

"That must be his wife," Nikki says. "And look at that dog. It's one of those scary kinds of dogs."

They follow along at a distance behind their substitute teacher. He looks so different right then, he could be a different person. They watch him laugh and then stoop to pet the top of his dangerous-looking dog's head. Nikki and Deja glance at each other. How is it that teachers look so different when they're not at school?

"You know what?" Nikki asks.

"What?"

"He should bring that dog to school tomorrow. Just let it sit in the back of the class. Then I betcha even the bad kids will be good."

Deja bursts into laughter picturing Carlos and Ralph and Richard and Ayanna and all of the bad kids sitting perfectly still with their hands folded and their eyes big with fear. Nikki joins her, and they laugh all the way to Mr. Delvecchio's.

The next morning Nikki and Deja arrive at school early because Nikki's mom has a dentist appointment and is able to give them a ride. As soon as they enter the schoolyard, they see four or five boys from their class in an excited huddle next to the handball court.

"What's going on with them?" Nikki asks, squinting.

Deja shrugs. "Let's go find out." She leads the way. But she doesn't walk directly up to the group. She sits down on the bench next to the court and the group of boys, and reaches down to tie her shoe. "Your shoe's untied too, Nikki."

Nikki looks down. Her shoes have Velcro. But

she sits down and pretends to do something with the Velcro strap. From their vantage point, they can hear the boys clearly. The boys are so excited they don't even notice Nikki and Deja. Instead they're busy interrupting each other, trying to squeeze in their own ideas for that day's fun at Mr. Willow's expense.

Nikki and Deja stop pretending to tie their shoes and just sit and listen unnoticed.

"This is what we do," Ralph says. "When it's morning-journal time and it's all quiet and stuff, we all wait until the big hand gets on the twelve, then I drop my math book. Then when the big hand gets on the one, Carlos drops his book. When it gets on the two, Richard drops his book. Then, when it gets on the three, we all drop our books."

Ralph looks around and they suddenly all burst into laughter. "This is going to be good!" Carlos says.

"Let's think of something else, for after re- cess," Willis says. He's another new boy from a school across town.

"That Willis probably got kicked out of his old school," Nikki whispers to Deja.

"Yeah," Deja says, looking over at him. She doesn't like what she sees. His shirt is already hanging out, and school hasn't even started yet.

"I know," Willis says breathlessly. "My old teacher really hated when we would move our chairs, because it made a lot of noise until she bought a bunch of tennis balls and put them on the chair legs. So I'll scoot my chair like I'm trying to get comfortable, and then when I finish, you can scoot yours," he says, pointing to Carlos. "And then you can do it," he says, pointing to Richard. "And then you," he adds, pointing to Ralph.

"I betcha he did all kinds of bad things at his old school," Deja says.

"Yeah," Nikki agrees.

The lineup bell rings then. Nikki and Deja try to find their places, but it's hard because so many of the kids have just lined up wherever they please. There's a lot of laughing going on. Deja's place in line has been behind Keisha, but Keisha is in the back of the line talking to her friend Ayanna. Nikki's place in line is behind Casey, but Rosario has taken Casey's place. The boys are equally mixed up, and loving it. It's a mess.

"Where's Mr. *Wiiiillllloooww?*" Keisha asks in that new drawn-out way a lot of the kids have adopted.

"Yeah," Rosario says, looking around. "Where's Mr. *Wiiiilllllloooww?*"

"I wish he'd come up here with that dog of

his," Deja says under her breath. She watches the other classes walking in orderly lines toward the school building. She looks around. No Mr. Willow. She glances over at Nikki. Nikki does a little shrug and looks around too.

Carlos begins the chant: "Where's Mr. *Wiiiilllllloooww?* Where's Mr. *Wiiiilllllloooww?* Where's Mr. *Wiiiilllllloooww?*" Everyone — except the good kids — joins in.

That Willis character calls out, "He's afraid to come to school!" He doubles over with laughter, and several of the boys and girls near him join in.

6

Meet Mr. Blaggart

Across the yard, Deja spots a figure walking toward them. No, more like marching toward them. All the other classes have gone into the school building. Room Ten is the only class still left on the yard. The figure gets closer. It's a man. Kind of a big man. A man she has never seen before. Is he a new sub? The boisterous kids don't notice. They're too busy being loud.

But Richard notices — and then Antonia, and Casey, and then Beverly and Erik and that kind-of-new boy, Gavin. They all see the man with the no-nonsense look coming right at them. He gets closer and finally plants himself in front of the straggly line with his head forward on his thick neck, eyes bugged out big as golf balls, and furry brows that are sunk down and meeting like two caterpillars shaking hands.

He stands there looking at them. Then he squints, surveying the line.

One by one, the students grow quiet — some out of curiosity, some out of fear, Deja guesses. Soon everyone is paying attention to the man standing in front of them. He's not a giant, but he gives the impression of being one. He's taller and bulkier than Mr. Willow, and he has one of those haircuts that makes his hair look like sharp, short bristles sticking up out of his head. His hands look like huge paws hanging at his sides. Big bear paws. Deja realizes she feels a tiny bit of fear too. He just stands there, looking over the class. Then he moves his hands behind him and stands like a soldier. "Follow me! And no laggers, or you're going to get an extra lap!"

Willis, in front of her, nudges Carlos, in front of him. They smile at each other and then look back at the new sub. *They don't have any sense,* Deja thinks. Can't they see that this sub is *not* Mr. Willow?

He leads them to the lunch tables and benches. "Find a seat!"

Everyone eventually finds a seat. Carlos and Richard sit side by side and immediately begin elbowing each other. The new teacher swivels his head around and glares at them. He points at them with one big sausage finger.

"You two!" he says. "Drop your backpacks and give me three laps around this schoolyard. The rest of you, give me two laps! This is called our morning constitutional, and we'll be doing this every morning to get us ready for a *hard day of learning!*"

Most of the kids look like they don't know what to think. One by one they come up with their backpacks, place them on the lunch tables, and start for the edge of the playground.

"I don't want to see any walking! I see walking and you get another lap! And after you finish, line up right here!" He points his finger down at the spot in front of him.

As soon as the students from Room Ten enter their classroom, they start whispering complaints to each other. "This teacher is *mean,*" Rosario says, looking back over her shoulder at him. He stands just inside the door, checking a clipboard.

"I'm waiting for everyone to close their mouths and listen up!" the new substitute says, not shouting, but in a very *strong* voice.

Rosario rolls her eyes at Keisha. Keisha sucks her teeth just as the sub turns in her direction.

There's a little gasp from Beverly, who's easily rattled.

The new sub walks directly over to Keisha. She is turned away, whispering something to Rosario behind her hand. He stands right in front of Keisha. She drops her hand and looks up at him.

"Do you speak English?" he asks her.

Deja's mouth drops open at this point. *Uh-oh,* she thinks. Keisha has been known to be a little bit sassy. Not to Ms. Shelby-Ortiz, but to past substitutes.

This time, she seems to know that sassy is not the way to go. "Yes," she mumbles.

"I didn't hear you," the sub says, his voice low and scary.

"Yes, I said, I speak English."

"Do you have trouble hearing, then?"

"No."

"Then you heard me tell everyone to close their mouths?"

Keisha doesn't say anything. She just looks down.

"I'm sorry," he says, not sounding at all sorry. "I didn't hear you."

"Yes, I heard you," she says quietly.

"Listen up!" he says to everyone. "You have five minutes to put away your stuff and get in your seats. Five minutes," he repeats sharply. Most of the students speed up their morning routine. But there are four or five Knucklehead Club members who pay no attention to the fact that there's been a change in Room Ten.

Carlos still sits at what is really Ayanna's desk, and Ayanna takes her place next to her best friend, Rosario, at Carlos's desk. The new sub goes immediately to the board and writes his name in huge letters: **MR. BLAGGART.**

Deja stares at it for a few seconds. "Mr. Blaggart," she mouths. She looks over at Nikki. She's mouthing it as well. Deja's never heard of that name before. But it sounds . . . it sounds . . . it sounds *mean.* She studies Mr. Blaggart. He's still checking a paper on a clipboard in his hand. Then he turns and starts drawing a floor plan of the classroom on the whiteboard. That catches some of the kids' attention. They sit quietly, waiting. They watch him fill in their clusters of desks. Slowly, what noisiness there is dies down. Everyone turns to the board, curious to see what this Mr. Blaggart person is doing. Mr. Blaggart finishes drawing and looks over the class. His eyes seem to lock with each of theirs for just a few seconds. It's as if he can look right through them.

"Now," he says, "I'm Mr. *Blaggart.*" He speaks

forcefully, and Carlos and Ralph look at each other and smirk. Mr. Blaggart sees them. "Did I say something funny?"

No response.

"Stand up, you two!"

Carlos and Ralph stand.

"I'll ask you again." Now he lowers his voice and says in a kind of hiss, *"Did I say something funny?"*

"No," Carlos says in a near whisper.

"I can't hear you," Mr. Blaggart says, then looks over at Ralph.

"No," Ralph says.

He's like a drill sergeant, Deja thinks. Like in a movie she saw once on TV.

"Sit down," he orders.

They sit.

"First thing," he continues, "I'm going to call your tables *teams!* Team One, Team Two, Team Three, Team Four, and Team Five." He points at them as he names them. Right after he's pointed to Team Five, Carlos blurts out, "But that's Table One!"

Everyone quickly looks to Mr. Blaggart to see what he's going to do. Mr. Blaggart turns to Carlos and looks at him for a long moment . . . a really long moment. Carlos seems to wither under it. He drops his eyes.

"Take out your morning journals," Mr. Blaggart says. "While I take the roll using your teacher's seating chart, let's have Ayanna suggest a topic to write about." He looks directly at Carlos.

Ayanna's eyes dart from Mr. Blaggart to Carlos and then back at Carlos again.

"Ayanna, do you have a topic you'd like to suggest to the class?" he asks Carlos.

Carlos begins to frown. He looks confused.

"Ayanna?" Mr. Blaggart repeats. He crosses the room to stand right next to Carlos.

Richard begins to snicker. Then Rosario joins in. Mr. Blaggart looks over at them. They stop. Then he turns to Ayanna, who's started to join in the laughter. "What about you, Carlos? Do you have a topic you'd like to suggest?"

She stops abruptly and looks over at Carlos.

"Carlos?" Mr. Blaggart asks again.

Ayanna shakes her head and looks down.

Antonia raises her hand then. Mr. Blaggart notices and nods his head.

"Maybe we can write about why it's important for everyone to follow rules — especially rules set up by their teacher. Even when there's a sub."

"I like that," Mr. Blaggart says readily. His eyes rest on Carlos. "Ayanna, is that all right with you?"

"My name isn't Ayanna," Carlos says boldly.

"It isn't?" Mr. Blaggart walks quickly to Ms. Shelby-Ortiz's desk and picks up her clipboard. He makes a show of consulting it and looking around the room. He looks up at the whiteboard and then back at Carlos. He frowns and looks at the whiteboard again. "No, I'm sure that seat belongs to a student named Ayanna. So you must be Ayanna. That seat, according to your teacher, was given to Ayanna. I'm sure you wouldn't sit in a seat that doesn't belong to you. Am I right, Carlos?" he asks, looking right at Ayanna.

Ayanna doesn't say anything. She clearly doesn't know what to say.

Mr. Blaggart repeats, "Am I right?"

"This is Carlos's seat," she says, giving in quickly and in a near whisper, as if she doesn't want the class to hear her. "Carlos is in my seat."

"I see," Mr. Blaggart says. "Then what should you and Carlos do, at this point?"

Everyone is watching her intently. Deja bets they're all super glad they aren't Ayanna — or Carlos.

Mr. Blaggart swivels to Carlos, who seems to be trying to look completely innocent. "What do you think?"

Carlos doesn't say anything.

Mr. Blaggart moves to Carlos and stares down

at him. "What do you think, Carlos?" His voice sounds a little bit louder.

"I have to move to my own seat," Carlos says quietly.

"Excellent," Mr. Blaggart says with a huge grin on his face, just like the cat in *Alice in Wonderland*, the one with the big piano-key teeth.

Deja stares at that smile. Mr. Blaggart actually does have teeth that look like piano keys.

Now Ayanna begins taking all of her books, and her pencil case, and her Ziploc bag of markers and crayons, and an empty bag of potato chips (that she balls up quickly and stuffs into her pocket) out of Carlos's desk.

The whole class, including Carlos, watches her. Then Carlos scoots his chair back and stretches himself out so the back of his head is resting on the back of his chair. He raises his eyebrows.

Meekly, Ayanna, with her arms full of her things, walks across the room to where Carlos is sitting. She stands there waiting for him to get up. When he doesn't move, she lets her books and all her other stuff slide out of her arms and onto the desk.

Carlos *tsk*s loudly. He stands and begins gathering his belongings from inside the desk. When

his arms are crammed full of books and small toys and spiral notebooks and pencils, he starts across the room toward the seat assigned to him by his teacher. But Mr. Blaggart stops him.

"Oh, no, buddy boy. You look like you need some time alone — to think and get rid of your attitude. I want you to sit at the special desk by the class library." Carlos stops in his tracks. He pivots dramatically and, nearly stomping his feet as he walks, heads in the direction of what everyone calls the dummy desk. It's where you go when you're having problems following directions. It's where you go when you need to do your work by yourself — where there are no distractions, and where the teacher can keep a close eye on you. It's where you go so that you will not disturb others who are trying to stay on task and do their own work.

Deja can see that Nikki is trying to stifle a laugh. Keisha is trying to keep from laughing as well.

Mr. Blaggart claps a loud, thunderous clap. Then he walks over to the whiteboard and writes the topic for their morning journals in giant letters: **WHY IT'S IMPORTANT TO FOLLOW RULES!**

"Okay, everybody. Let's get to work!" He looks around the room as everyone pulls out his or her journal and slowly gets to work. When he seems satisfied, he settles in at Ms. Shelby-Ortiz's desk, picks up a newspaper he must have brought with him, snaps it open, and begins to read.

Deja is shocked. Ms. Shelby-Ortiz would never do such a thing. Read a newspaper? Deja's sure there's a rule against such a thing. But Mr. Blaggart looks perfectly at ease breaking it.

7

Blaggart Days

Later, when Deja looks around, nearly everyone is working. There are only a few slackers. Keisha is staring into space. That new boy Willis is drawing in his journal, and Ralph is playing with some tiny action figures he has in his desk. His journal sits closed next to them.

After a few moments of trying to think of something to write, Deja puts the date on her page in the upper right corner, just like Ms. Shelby-Ortiz tells them to do. Then she writes the journal topic on the top line. She stares at it. She looks over at Nikki, already knowing Nikki is having no problem writing, since she wants to be a journalist when she grows up. She's probably written a whole page already. Deja begins with something kind of stupid-sounding:

We have to have rules in this school and in this world, too. If there were no rules on the street, cars could crash into each other because they'd go on the red and maybe stop on the green if they felt like it, and people would just butt in the lunch line and people would just throw their paper towels on the floor in the restroom instead of in the trash can. And kids wouldn't do their homework and kids would come to school anytime they wanted and . . .

Feeling eyes in her direction, Deja looks up. Mr. Blaggart is looking right at Ralph, who is so engrossed in his playing, he doesn't notice. But he must suddenly feel the pressure of Mr. Blaggart's stare, because he looks up and then quietly slides all the toys back inside his desk. Then he carefully pulls his journal to himself and opens it. He looks up at Mr. Blaggart. The teacher is still staring at him. His caterpillar eyebrows have knitted together. He's so scary, Deja has to look away.

Ralph starts writing, making Deja wonder what he could have come up with so immediately. Mr. Blaggart stands and casually starts moving in Ralph's direction. It's just like a tiger moving in for the kill. Ralph keeps writing — Deja can't imagine what. Mr. Blaggart comes to stand right next to his desk. He folds his arms and reads over Ralph's shoulder. Ralph stops writing.

Mr. Blaggart begins to read aloud: "'We need rules. We need rules. We need rules. We need rules. We need rules. We need rules.'. . . Well, well, well. What's that about, Ralph?"

Ralph seems to flinch at the sound of his name coming out of Mr. Blaggart's mouth. "I dunno," he says, finally.

"Well, Ralph, do you know what Mr. Blaggart thinks?"

Ralph gives one quick shake of his head.

"I think you've already had your recess playing with whatever you've been playing with in your desk. I think you can stay in from recess and write about why it's important to follow rules. But I think you should add to that and write about the importance of doing your best, too. What do you think? Does that sound like a good idea?"

"Yes," Ralph says in a quiet voice.

Then Mr. Blaggart holds out his big fat palm.

Ralph stares at it, puzzled. Then the reason dawns on him. He reaches into his desk and extracts three action figures. He hands them over.

"Thanks," Mr. Blaggart says, taking them. He holds out his other hand, smiling down at Ralph.

Ralph frowns a little, then reaches way into his desk and takes out three more figures. He hands them over. Mr. Blaggart puts them in the fist that grips the other figures and holds out his empty palm again.

Ralph sighs and gathers more figures and hands them over too.

"Class, who can tell me the rule about bringing toys to school?"

Beverly's hand shoots up.

Mr. Blaggart nods at her.

"Don't bring toys to school!" she says, projecting her voice.

"Right," Mr. Blaggart says. "Otherwise they go in my special box" — he indicates a box on top of the file cabinet, one they've never seen before — "and then they go with me to Goodwill at the end of the day. I know there are some nice little kids who will be thrilled to get the toys you bring from home."

The bell for morning recess rings then, and everyone breathes a sigh of relief. They can finally get away from mean Mr. Blaggart.

No one jumps up, though. They wait and wait.

"Team Two! Line up!"

Team Two sits stunned for a moment, as if they don't know what to do.

"Team Two!" Mr. Blaggart shouts.

All the students on Team Two get up, push their chairs under their desks, and nearly tiptoe to the door leading to the schoolyard. They stand there ramrod-straight, mouths zipped, eyes big.

"I like Team Two!" Mr. Blaggart says. He puts his hands on his hips. "Team Five!"

Quietly, Team Five gets up. Following Team Two's lead, they walk to the door with mouths closed and line up in a very orderly fashion behind Team Two. Next he chooses Team Three, then Team One, and last, Team Four.

On the yard in the handball line, Deja overhears Ralph tell Carlos, "That teacher doesn't scare me."

"He doesn't scare me, either," Carlos says.

"Me, neither," Willis chimes in. "Let's do the book-dropping thing after recess."

Carlos doesn't say anything.

"What — are you scared?"

"No, not really," Carlos says, but he doesn't sound as bold as he did earlier when he thought they'd be ganging up on Mr. Willow.

"I'm not scared," Willis declares. "I'll go first,

even. When the big hand gets on the six. Who goes after me?" He looks from Carlos to Ralph to Richard, and then back to Carlos.

"I'll go next," Richard says. "And Carlos, you next, and then Ralph. We drop our books every five minutes."

Deja can't help thinking, *Oh, I wouldn't do that if I were you.* . . . But she stays out of it. She has to admit she's almost looking forward to the trouble they're going to bring on themselves.

The second bell has rung and now all the students run to their lines to wait for their teachers. Across the yard, Deja sees Mr. Blaggart walking toward them. He's wearing glasses he didn't have on before. When he reaches their line, he says in a chilly voice, "I want everyone to make sure . . ." He stops and looks over his glasses at each of them, it seems. ". . . I want every student to get in the place assigned to you by your teacher."

At first, everyone remains in place. Some kids probably don't want Mr. Blaggart to know that they've taken advantage of Ms. Shelby-Ortiz's absence, Deja guesses. He looks down at his scary clipboard and then looks up at Keisha, who's standing behind her best friend, Rosario. Sheepishly, she gets out of the line and then gets back in behind Beverly. Mr. Blaggart looks at Carlos, and Carlos moves back to his place at the end of the line. That starts up more kids getting out of the line and then getting back in at the right place. Soon all the students are where they *should* be. Mr. Blaggart leads the line to the classroom.

Once the class is settled at their *assigned* desks, Mr. Blaggart points to the whiteboard. "Gavin, please read the assignment I've written there."

In a quiet voice, Gavin says, "Read the story on page forty-three in the anthology. Answer the questions on page fifty-four. Use complete sentences in your answers."

"Any questions?" Mr. Blaggart asks. He looks around the room, his eyes big and scary. Then he strides like a soldier to Ms. Shelby-Ortiz's desk, sits down, and opens his newspaper. His face is hidden behind the paper, but Deja bets his hearing is as sharp as a dog's.

She looks around. Carlos is giving Willis a little nod. Deja looks at the clock. It's twenty-five after ten. She remembers their silly plan. She opens her book to page forty-three.

Deja has almost forgotten about their plan when she hears the first book drop. There's a loud *thud.* Students look up from their desks. Mr.

Blaggart looks over at Willis. Everyone quickly gets back to work. But Mr. Blaggart doesn't take his eyes off Willis. In fact, he gives him a little smile. Willis looks puzzled. He picks up his book and, acting innocent, gets back to work.

Just after the big hand clicks to the seven on the clock above the whiteboard, there's another loud *thud*. Everyone looks over at Richard. He bends down to pick up his book. Deja checks Mr. Blaggart. This time he only glances up, looks over at Richard, and then back down at his newspaper.

Deja and Nikki finish their work at the same time. Deja closes her book, raises her hand, and waves it until Mr. Blaggart looks up and nods.

"Can I go to the puzzle table and work on our class puzzle?" Ms. Shelby-Ortiz always lets them work on the seven-hundred-piece puzzle of New York City if they finish their work before the rest of the class.

They'd already finished an eight-hundred-piece rain forest puzzle earlier that year. Ms. Shelby-Ortiz got it framed, and now it hangs on the wall next to their class library.

Deja loves working on a jigsaw puzzle. She finds it challenging and thrilling, and a great way to be able to talk quietly in class.

"Bring your workbook up here and let me take a look," Mr. Blaggart orders.

Deja swallows hard. What if she hasn't done her work correctly? Since she was in a hurry to finish first, her handwriting isn't her best. She takes a deep breath and brings her workbook to Mr. Blaggart. She hands it over and watches him check her work very carefully.

"I'm not liking this handwriting," he says curtly. "Get some paper and rewrite these answers. This is unacceptable." He goes back to his newspaper.

Deja can't believe it. Ms. Shelby-Ortiz has never had her rewrite her workbook answers. The class just goes over the answers when everyone is finished. Perfect handwriting is for their compositions, not their workbooks. It's not fair.

Just then there's another loud *thud*. Deja turns around to see Carlos bending to pick up his book off the floor. She looks at Mr. Blaggart, but he's still reading his newspaper. She takes her workbook and slinks back to her seat.

"He's making you write your answers again?" Nikki whispers.

Deja looks over at Mr. Blaggart to make sure his head is still behind his newspaper.

"All of them. He said my handwriting isn't good enough."

Nikki, Beverly, and Erik look closely at their own handwriting. They start erasing and rewriting.

8

Benched

Mr. Blaggart has posted the day's schedule on the side of the whiteboard. Deja is happy to see that he's following Ms. Shelby-Ortiz's usual schedule. Today there's P.E. after math. Deja loves P.E. because that's when they have their team sports. She loves when it's her turn to be captain and she can choose her team. This week the team sport is kickball. She's good at rolling the ball for the kicker, and she's really good at kicking the ball — far!

In the afternoon, Deja can hardly get through math. She has to consult her multiplication fact sheet more than usual. She keeps looking at the clock, which seems to have slowed down. When she and most of the other students have placed their math papers in the in-box on Ms. Shelby-Ortiz's desk and have taken out their Sustained Silent Reading books, Deja still can't concentrate. She's just looking at the pages with her mind on other things.

Nikki coughs "the cough" to get Deja's attention. Deja reaches into the box to take out the note Nikki put there for her. It reads:

If you get to be captain, pick Rosario for your team. She kicks good.

As Deja folds the note to put it in her desk, she looks up to see Mr. Blaggart staring right at her. He's frowning and shaking his head slowly back and forth. Deja's mouth goes dry. Her heart speeds up. She looks over at Nikki, but Nikki is busy with her SSR. *Oh, no,* Deja thinks. But then she talks herself out of her fear. Maybe she's just imagining things. Maybe that frown on his face means nothing. She looks down at her Sustained Silent Reading book and begins to read.

Finally, Mr. Blaggart gets up and walks to the front of the class. "Put away your SSR books," he says. He has a stack of papers in his hand: their completed math papers. "When I call your name, line up." He looks at the papers in his hand and begins to call the names of those who've turned in their work.

Deja is surprised. She turned her paper in, but he doesn't call her name. Not hers or Nikki's. He doesn't call the names of Richard, Carlos, Ralph, and Willis, either. He doesn't call Beverly and Ayanna. This is obviously because they dilly-dallied and didn't complete their work. Actually, when have Beverly or Ayanna ever completed an assignment in a timely manner? Deja can see why their names weren't called.

Mr. Blaggart checks something on his clip-board.

"Gavin, you and Antonia are team captains. You may choose your teams."

Teams are chosen, and Mr. Blaggart has them line up at the door. "Carlos, Richard, Willis, and Ralph. All of you are benched for not being able to work without playing." Ralph starts to protest. Mr. Blaggart raises his furry eyebrows, and that stops Ralph cold.

"Ayanna and Beverly, you can do the work you didn't finish on the bench, so bring out your pencils and workbooks. And Nikki and Deja, you're benched for passing notes."

Deja's mouth drops open. She wants to say something, but she can't think of anything. She looks over at Nikki. Nikki's looking down with her mouth downturned as well, as if she might cry. *Nikki's so sensitive,* Deja thinks.

Nikki and Deja get in the back of the line and follow their classmates to the yard. While most of the students run to the kickball diamond, they walk to the lunch benches. With the *slowpokes* and the *knuckleheads.*

Deja doesn't mean to pay attention to the game, but it's exciting, with close scores, and it's something to do. Nikki watches forlornly, with her lower lip poked out. She *never* gets in trouble. This is probably a new experience for her.

Deja looks over at Mr. Blaggart. He's watching the game with a scowl on his face and his eternal clipboard in his hand. Every once in a while, over the least little squabble or disagreement about the score or who's out or who's going to roll the ball, he blasts his whistle and threatens to take them all back to the classroom for more math. Everyone gets it together then and the squabbles die down.

"It was one little note," Deja protests — again — as they walk home from school.

Nikki is silent. Then she says, "I'm just glad he didn't send us to the office."

"Nikki, nobody's going to be sent to the office for passing a note." Deja is surprised that Nikki doesn't know that. Nikki always takes things too much to heart.

"Can we walk Ms. P. again when we get home?" she asks, brightening.

Deja smiles. Just the mention of her new dog gives her a good feeling. "Probably," she says.

Auntie Dee is doing a twisty thing on her yoga mat when Deja walks in the front door. Deja drops her backpack by the staircase and waits. Then Auntie Dee switches and twists to the other side. Deja sighs. It's so hard to wait while Auntie Dee takes her time. She's been doing yoga at home with a DVD since she had to drop her yoga class to save money, but recently there has been a bit of good news. Auntie Dee might get her job back soon. That's put her in a super-good mood. Nevertheless, she doesn't like to be interrupted while she's doing her yoga or meditating.

Deja goes into the kitchen, washes her hands, and then digs into a box of cookies while Auntie Dee's attention is elsewhere. Suddenly she hears little Ms. P. in the backyard barking and running toward the house. Deja stuffs her mouth full of cookie and opens the back door.

"There you are," Deja says. "There's Ms. P.!" She squats down to stroke the top of Ms. P.'s

head and nuzzle her under her chin. Then she gives the little dog a big hug.

By the time Deja goes back inside, Auntie Dee is putting away her yoga mat.

"Can I take Ms. P. for a walk?"

"Sure. I didn't get a chance to walk her today."

Deja meets Nikki on the sidewalk out front. They take a new route this afternoon, but one that still takes them by Delvecchio's, this time for hot chips. Ms. P. trots along happily. They go toward Maynard and then up Ashby toward Marin. When they pass the cleaners, they see Mr. Blaggart coming out with a bunch of shirts on hangers and a few blouses in plastic.

"Mr. Blaggart," Nikki says in a whisper, as if someone can hear them.

"He must have a *wife*, or a daughter."

"Mr. Blaggart with a daughter?"

They watch him approach a blue sedan in the parking lot next to the cleaners. He hangs up the shirts and blouses on that hook thing above the rear driver window. Then he gets in his car and starts up the motor. They watch him drive away. It's so strange. . . . First they see Mr. Willow with a dog, then they see Mr. Blaggart picking up his dry cleaning. And once, they saw their beloved teacher, Ms. Shelby-Ortiz, in Food Barn buying regular stuff like yogurt and toothpaste.

It's weird to think of teachers having to go to the supermarket or to the cleaners. Or even having a dog.

As soon as they enter Delvecchio's, they see Richard and Willis from their class. Both are at the counter paying for sodas and chips. Willis is too busy talking to Richard to even notice Nikki and Deja. He's got more plots to set into motion. They're discussing the chair-scraping tactic. Apparently that's on the agenda for the next day, and a coughing fit, too.

"We'll do the chair-scraping before recess and the coughing thing after recess," Willis says.

"Yeah," Richard agrees. "That's going to be fun."

On the way home, Nikki announces, "We should write a letter to Mr. Blaggart and tell him that there's a whole bunch of stuff going on right under his nose. Stuff from kids who need to be benched for a month."

Deja thinks about this. She remembers how she got in trouble trying to get that Post-it note off Mr. Willow's jacket. She needs to think about Nikki's suggestion a little bit more. It could backfire. She digs her hand into her hot-chip bag and almost gives one to Ms. P. Then she thinks better of it. A dog probably wouldn't like a hot chip. She pushes a handful into her own mouth instead. She knows Auntie wouldn't like her eating all those artificial ingredients and that red dye in the hot chips. But they're so delicious.

She remembers the time Auntie pointed out the list of ingredients, asking her which ones she thought were real food.

"That stuff can't be good for you," Auntie Dee had declared.

But it sure tasted good, Deja had thought. Of course, she hadn't said it.

9

Come Back,
Ms. Shelby-Ortiz

The days go by in regimented fashion. On Thursday, the boys pull their chair-scraping routine, but it fizzles. Mr. Blaggart barely looks up. He just benches all the participants, with little explanation. "I don't have to tell you why you're being benched, now, do I?" he says. The glare in his eyes stops all protest.

Every morning, Mr. Blaggart marches to the line, leads the students to the lunch benches, and yells, "Listen up! Drop those backpacks and give me five laps." Everyone starts out in a big bunch. Soon, Beverly and a few resistant students, who don't see why they have to start each morning running around the schoolyard, lag behind. Some try to get away with a half-run, half-walk trot type of thing, but then there's a blast from Mr. Blaggart's whistle and they speed it up.

After the fifth lap, he blows his whistle again and tells everyone to line up at the door of the building and get ready to work, work, work.

On Friday, the morning-journal topic is *Why Work Is Good!*

There's a little groan from someone, then Beverly whispers, "How come we never get to have open topics like with Ms. Shelby-Ortiz?"

Deja gives a tiny shrug in response. She's too afraid to do more. But then she whispers, all the while keeping her eyes on Mr. Blaggart, "Because he's not Ms. Shelby-Ortiz."

"I can't wait until she comes back," Beverly says, a little too loudly for Deja's taste.

Deja says nothing but quickly looks over at Mr. Blaggart. Then she gets to work. She writes:

Work is good because it can be hard, and doing hard stuff can make you strong. My Auntie Dee loves to work. Right now she has to work at home because where she used to work they ran out of money and they had to let her go. When I grow up I want to work. But I want to have kids too, so I want to do both. I want to be a decorator. I want to go into people's

houses and tell them what they did
wrong with their decorating like if
they have colors that clash or old
fashioned furniture or if they keep
their rooms too dark like a lot of old
people. I have a neighbor. She's old and
you have to turn on the lights in the
daytime at her house and

Deja looks at Mr. Blaggart. He's gotten up
from Ms. Shelby-Ortiz's desk and has started
walking slowly around the room. Like Mr.
Willow, he's got one of those thermal-cup things
in his hand. *Something Ms. Shelby-Ortiz would
never do,* Deja thinks disapprovingly.

Mr. Blaggart winds his way over to Willis. He
looks down at him and smiles. But it isn't a real
smile, Deja feels. There's a threat somewhere in
there. Mr. Blaggart takes a sip of his coffee and
moves on.

About forty seconds later, while Deja is busy
reading over what she's written and trying to
think of more, she hears the loud, squeaky scrape
of a chair. It's Ralph. He looks horrified, as if he's
afraid that accidental scrape might seem as if
it was done on purpose. He looks over at Mr.
Blaggart, who acts as if he hasn't heard anything.

He's back at Ms. Shelby-Ortiz's desk, reading his newspaper.

Deja finishes up her journal entry and puts it away.

"Ralph," Mr. Blaggart says in a booming voice, "go to the front of the class, please, and take your journal with you."

Ralph stands up slowly, frowning. He closes his journal and brings it up to the front of the room.

"Everyone, quiet. Let's listen to Ralph read his entry."

Suddenly, Ralph looks concerned. His eyes get all shifty and he has a little frown on his face. He takes a long time finding his entry. He flips pages back and forth.

Stalling, Deja thinks.

He finally comes to the page and brings the book up to his face so he's practically hiding behind it. From behind his rather messy-looking journal comes a mumbling, stumbling voice. Deja can't even make out what he's saying. Neither can Mr. Blaggart, apparently, because he walks over to Ralph and lowers his journal so all can see Ralph's mouth. Ralph then has a problem reading his own handwriting. Deja can never understand how someone can write something and then not be able to read it. But there's Ralph, standing up there in front of everyone, squinting at his own words as if he's never seen them before.

"'Every ... Everyone ...' No, I mean, 'Everybody has to work because everbody,' I mean, 'Everybody has to work ...'"

There is a long pause while he squints at his journal page. Deja yawns and looks around the room. Beverly is looking at Ralph with her mouth hanging open. Rosario is drawing hearts on her journal cover, Richard is playing with the zipper on his jacket (which he should have hung up on the peg below his cubby), and Mr. Blaggart is standing there with his arms folded, waiting. Ralph continues:

"'... to get money to buy things like (*squint, squint*) food!'"

The class waits for the rest of Ralph's entry. Silence. He closes his journal and looks at Mr. Blaggart.

"Is that it?" Mr. Blaggart asks from the back of the room.

"Yes," Ralph declares, as if that's a reasonable answer.

"Even though you've been writing for the last twenty minutes?"

Ralph doesn't answer.

"You can finish it during recess." Mr. Blaggart looks around as if he's trying to decide who should go next. Suddenly, Deja wishes he would pick her. Hers would sound so good in comparison to Ralph's. It's all she can do to keep her hand down.

"Richard," Mr. Blaggart announces.

Richard looks up, surprised. Slowly, he picks up his journal. Slowly, he gets out of his seat. Slowly, he walks to the front of the class. He takes even more time than Ralph in finding the right page. When he finds it, he stands there staring at it. The class waits. Mr. Blaggart waits. After a few moments of watching Richard staring at his page, Mr. Blaggart walks toward him and looks over his shoulder at the journal page. He takes it out of Richard's hand and holds it up to the class. Blank. Some kids start laughing. Some look down at their own journals and immediately start adding to their entries.

The recess bell rings then, and Mr. Blaggart moves to the door. "Pencils down," he orders, and looks around the room to see that all pencils are down. Deja smiles at her nearly full page of writing. She looks at Nikki, who has a smug smile on her face as well.

"When I call your team number, open your

journals to today's date and bring them up here and get in line." Everyone straightens up then. "Team One!"

Team One lines up at the door with their open journals.

"Team Two!"

When all the teams—excluding Ralph and Richard—are lined up at the door with their open journals, Mr. Blaggart goes down the line checking them. "You go back to your desk and start writing," he says to Keisha. "You, too," he says to Carlos. Willis and Rosario have to go back to their desks as well. The rest of the students are dimissed after they stack their journals in the classwork tray.

The grumbling starts immediately and continues all the way to the handball court.

"That teacher is *mean*," Ayanna says. "I can't wait until Ms. Shelby-Ortiz comes back."

"I'm sick of having to do all that running first thing in the morning," says Antonia.

"Maybe if we're extra bad, he'll leave just like Mr. Willow," Casey suggests.

"He's not Mr. Willow," Deja reminds them. She doesn't think anything could scare Mr. Blaggart away.

"I wish Ms. Shelby-Ortiz's ankle would hurry up and heal. She's way better," Ayanna says.

Then Ayanna begins chanting, "Come back, Ms. Shelby-Ortiz. Come back, Ms. Shelby-Ortiz." Soon everyone has joined in. But not too loudly, in case Mr. Blaggart is lurking about.

There's a list of words on the board, all beginning with *W.* Mr. Blaggart has put the long list there for them to alphabetize. He has probably done this to keep them busy while he sips his coffee and reads his paper. It's going to be torture because the words all begin with the same letter. The students will have to look at the second letter to see where each word goes, and then if there is more than one word with the first and second letters alike, they'll have to look at the third letter. It's all so confusing and boring.

Deja sighs—but quietly. Nikki has already taken out her paper and numbered it. *Oh, when will this day end?* Deja thinks as she begins to number her paper. She just wants to get home, have her snack, and walk Ms. Precious Penelope.

10

Dear
Ms. Shelby-Ortiz

The boring and grim routine continues: morning constitutionals; journal writing (while Mr. Blaggart reads his newspaper); reading and answering questions in excellent handwriting to the sound of Mr. Blaggart turning his newspaper pages and working the crossword puzzle; then recess, which brings a little relief. Then there's more work and all with *no talking!* It's so boring, Deja can hardly take it. Plus, all the students are afraid to even move their chairs or cough, thanks to the Knucklehead Club.

When is Ms. Shelby-Ortiz coming back? Deja wonders for the hundredth time. It's been more than two weeks!

Deja considers complaining to Auntie Dee, but then thinks that Auntie Dee might like Mr.

Blaggart's way of doing things. Especially if she tells Auntie about the antics the bozos tried to pull the first few days.

The week before, having *not* learned his lesson, Richard broke his pencil lead. He requested permission to get another one. Mr. Blaggart let him come up to the desk for a fresh pencil from the pencil box once, but when Richard broke the lead a second time, he got a crayon to use for the rest of the day. That was funny, Deja thought, and it cured everyone of breaking pencil leads on purpose.

On Tuesday, as if he just can't help himself, Willis starts up with some fake-sounding coughing. Mr. Blaggart lets him do that all he wants, but then he has Willis sit on the bench to "rest" for morning recess, lunch recess, *and* during P.E. That cures him of his cough. Later that day, when Carlos scoots his chair a little bit too much, Mr. Blaggart has him complete his work standing up.

On Friday, Deja goes to the office with the lunch count. Mr. Blaggart has made her lunch monitor. He stopped following Ms. Shelby-Ortiz's way of doing things after the first few days. He just calls out a name and has that person pass out paper or pencils or books, or go to the office, or whatever.

While she is waiting for Mrs. Marker to take the lunch count out of her hand, Deja sees an envelope addressed to Ms. Shelby-Ortiz sitting in a basket at the end of the counter. It looks like it could be another get-well card, maybe from the other teachers. Deja stares at it. She examines the address. Jacaranda Lane! Ms. Shelby-Ortiz lives on Jacaranda Lane. *Fifty-two eleven* Jacaranda Lane! *Fifty-two eleven, fifty-two eleven, fifty-two eleven,* Deja says to herself over and over. It will be easy to memorize *Jacaranda Lane* because jacaranda trees with their beautiful lavender flowers are Deja's favorite trees. She can easily imagine a lane lined with jacaranda trees on both sides, and at the end of that lane, her dear teacher's house.

Finally, Mrs. Marker comes to the counter and takes the lunch-count folder out of Deja's hand.

All the way back to Room Ten, Deja says under her breath, *Fifty-two eleven, fifty-two eleven, fifty-two eleven.* When she returns to her seat, she can barely focus her attention on her multiplication fact sheet. Mr. Blaggart is letting them study their facts before a quiz. Those who can prove they've mastered their next table can then participate in P.E. Those who haven't will have to bring their fact sheets out to the yard and sit at the lunch table and study some more. Deja's on sevens. Those are hard. Nikki's on eights. Deja looks over at Nikki. She's putting her hand over the answers and testing herself.

It's so hard not to tell Nikki what she's found out. She could just burst. She stares at her sevens table and pictures herself out on the yard studying. Why couldn't she still be on fives?

Mr. Blaggart soon has Beverly pass out the Facts Quizzes face-down. Everyone knows they're only required to do the facts they haven't mastered yet. Poor Ralph has been on fours for the last three weeks. He must not be studying. Deja's been on sevens for just two weeks, but she's suddenly feeling confident. She glances over at Ralph just as he looks down at a cheat sheet on his lap. Deja's mouth drops open. *Is he crazy? Has he lost his mind? He's going to get caught and then . . .* Deja doesn't even want to think about it.

Mr. Blaggart rings Ms. Shelby-Ortiz's bell and they're off to the races. They have thirty seconds to finish their tables. Thirty seconds is really a lot of time, if you know the facts. Deja finishes with seconds to spare. Mr. Blaggart has Beverly collect the papers. He moves to the big Facts Quiz chart on the wall and starts with Casey. He checks her gold star in the eights column, then checks her paper. "Line up," he tells her. Casey has made it to nines. Deja is only interested in her own paper, though.

It takes a while to get to it. Finally, Mr. Blaggart has her paper in his hand. He checks the chart on the wall, sees that Deja is on sevens, checks her paper, and tells her to line up. She did it! She made it to eights! What a relief.

When he's gone through every paper, Ralph sheepishly raises his hand.

"Yes, Ralph?" Mr. Blaggart says.

Oh, no, Deja thinks.

"You didn't do my paper."

"You mean the paper that was on your lap?"

Ralph drops his eyes, and Deja, surprisingly, feels sorry for him. Why doesn't he just study?

Shockingly, Mr. Blaggart says only, "You're on the bench." Deja wonders why he doesn't seem angrier. Is Mr. Blaggart going soft? Does he even *have* a soft side?

She thinks about this all the way to the kickball diamond. Mr. Blaggart — a soft side? She thinks about seeing him at the cleaners, about him having a wife or a daughter. She still can't quite imagine it. But then she remembers: *Jacaranda Lane.*

"I know Ms. Shelby-Ortiz's address!" she says to Nikki while they stand in line waiting for their turn to kick.

"How?" Nikki asks.

"When I was in the office, I saw a piece of her mail."

"Did you write it down?"

"I didn't have to. I have it memorized. Fifty-two eleven Jacaranda Lane."

"I know where that is," Nikki says. "My cousin lives on that street. It's on the other side of the mall. Wow. We know where Ms. Shelby-Ortiz lives."

"Let's send her a get-well card," Nikki says on the way home.

"But we already sent her cards from the class. And what if she gets mad that we know where she lives?"

"We can send it anonymous," Deja says. "She won't even know it's from us."

Together, they walk Ms. P. up and down the block a few times. Then Deja puts her in the backyard and they settle on Nikki's porch to write a letter to Ms. Shelby-Ortiz. After a while they come up with this:

Dear Ms. Shelby-Ortiz,

How are you? We hope you're doing better. We hope you come back to school real soon because we've been having subs that are nothing like you and we miss you so, so, so, so, so much. Because you do everything just right and our class is better with you in it being our teacher. Ms. Shelby-Ortiz, please come back. If you can't walk we'll do everything for you. You can even teach us sitting down in a chair and we'll be so good. If you just come back.

Sincerely,
Anonymous

"I think it's just right," Nikki says.

Deja agrees. "I'll ask Auntie Dee to mail it for us tonight."

On the way to school the next morning, they decide not to tell anyone that they know where Ms. Shelby-Ortiz lives and that they sent her a letter asking her to hurry back. Everyone will just start begging for the address.

Something is different in the air when they reach the schoolyard, Deja notices. Something peaceful.

The class lines up neatly, all the students in their spots, mouths shut. Even the four knuckleheads, Willis, Richard, Carlos, and Ralph, are standing relatively still and keeping their hands to themselves. Everyone is nicely waiting for Mr. Blaggart to march them to the lunch benches to put down their backpacks so they can start their *morning constitutional.*

While she is standing there, Deja thinks how nice it would be if Mr. Blaggart finally gave them *Open Topic* for their morning-journal writing. She imagines what she'd write. It would be about Ms. Shelby-Ortiz. She'd write about why she misses Ms. Shelby-Ortiz, and she'd entitle it "Ten Reasons Why I Love Ms. Shelby-Ortiz":

One: She's nice.

Two: She's fair to everybody.

Three: It's fun saying her new name.

Four: She has pretty clothes.

Five: She has a really good grab bag that's full of interesting stuff, not just pencils and erasers.

Six: She lets us have pizza parties when we've been good for a while.

Seven: She never yells.

Eight: She wants us to do well.

Nine: She lets us sit with our friends if we can stay on task.

Ten: She likes us. All of us. Even when some of us are bad.

Deja has a tiny smile on her face thinking about her list. She looks around the yard. The sky is blue and the clouds are fat and fluffy. There's a slight breeze, and Auntie relented and put a regular brownie in her lunch as a special treat. Not one of those gluten-free, sweetened-with-applesauce brownies. As she thinks about it, she notices a small figure slowly crossing the yard, coming their way. Deja shields her eyes. It looks like Ms. Shel— Could that be Ms. Shelby-Ortiz slowly making her way toward them? Could that really be their beloved teacher, on

crutches, coming their way after more than two long weeks? She has her teacher bag over her shoulder, the one with the long strap.

Ralph breaks out of the line and rushes to help her. Carlos follows. Deja thinks she might be about to cry. That's how happy she feels. She looks over at Nikki. She has a big surprised look in her eyes and wears a huge grin. Deja looks at all her other classmates. Some seem as if they're in a trance. Then someone — Keisha, Deja thinks — starts chanting, "Ms. Shelby-Ortiz! Ms. Shelby-Ortiz!!!" Everyone joins in, and as their wonderful teacher hobbles toward them with her "helpers" beside her, the chant grows and grows until it fills the entire yard of George Washington Carver Elementary School.